THIS WALKER BOOK BELONGS TO:

Jessica

Cowan x

Cowen

For Sally, who likes fruit
H.C.

First published 1999 by Walker Books Ltd
87 Vauxhall Walk, London SE11 5HJ

This edition published 2004

2 4 6 8 10 9 7 5 3 1

Text © 1999 Joyce Dunbar
Illustrations © 1999 Helen Craig Ltd

The right of Joyce Dunbar and Helen Craig to be identified
as author and illustrator respectively of this work has been
asserted by them in accordance with the Copyright,
Designs and Patents Act 1988

This book has been typeset in Alpha Normal

Printed in China

British Library Cataloguing in Publication Data:
a catalogue record for this book is
available from the British Library

ISBN 0-7445-6389-5

www.walkerbooks.co.uk

PaNDa and Gander

Tutti-Frutti

Joyce Dunbar illustrated by Helen Craig

WALKER BOOKS
AND SUBSIDIARIES
LONDON • BOSTON • SYDNEY • AUCKLAND

Panda and Gander had a big bowl
of fruit to share.
"Tutti-frutti," said Panda.
"Frutti-tutti," said Gander.

Panda took a pear.

Gander took a pomegranate.

"I like a pear," said Panda.

"And I like a pomegranate," said Gander.

"I like the way you can eat a pear,"
said Panda. "You can pull off the
stalk and eat it from the top."
"And I like the way you can eat a
pomegranate," said Gander. "You can
cut it in half and pick out the pips."

Panda pulled the stalk off his pear
and ate it from the top.

"All gone," said Panda.

Gander cut his pomegranate in half and
picked out the pips.

"Pomegranates are very pippy," said Gander.

Panda took a banana.

"I like the way you can eat a banana,"
said Panda. "You pull down the peel
so that it looks like wings."

"All gone," said Panda.

"Pomegranates are very picky,"
said Gander.

Panda took a satsuma.

"I like the way you can eat a satsuma," said Panda. "Slice by slice. Slice by slice is very nice."

"Pip by pip is very slow," said Gander.

"All gone," said Panda.

"Pippy and picky," said Gander.

Panda helped himself to an apple.

"I like the way you can eat an apple," said Panda. "Big crunchy bites round the middle."

"All gone," said Panda.

Gander was still picking pips.

"The red pips are very sweet. The yellow pith is very bitter."

Panda took some grapes.

"I like the way you can eat grapes,"
said Panda.

"You bite them off, one at a time."

"All gone," said Panda.

"I am putting all the pips in a pile,"
said Gander.

"So you are," said Panda.

"There's a pile of peel. There's a pile of pith.
There's a pile of pips," said Gander.

"Juicy red pips," said Panda.

"That's right," said Gander.

"Juicy red pips without pith," said Panda.

"That's right," said Gander.

"When I have put all the pips in a pile,
I shall eat them all in one go," said
Gander.

"Will you?" said Panda.

"Yes," said Gander. "And see, I have
nearly finished. Look, what a big pile
of pomegranate pips."

"I like what you can do with cherries," said Panda. "You can dangle them over your ears."

"I don't have the right kind of ears," said Gander.

"Well, dangle them somewhere else,"
said Panda.

"All right, when I have eaten my
pomegranate pips," said Gander.

Gander started to eat
his pomegranate pips.
He scooped and he
slurped and he
swallowed.

"What about me?" said Panda.

"What about you?" said Gander.

"I have given you a share of the cherries, you should give me a share of your pomegranate pips," said Panda.

"All right," said Gander. "If you
give me a share of the pear."

"It's all gone," said Panda.

"How about a share of the banana?"

"All gone," said Panda.

"How about a share of the satsuma?"

"That's all gone too," said Panda.

"All right, how about the apple and
the grapes?"

"All gone," said Panda.

"Well, you see these pomegranate pips?"
"Yes," said Panda.

"All gone!" said Gander. And he dangled
the cherries on his wellies.

WALKER BOOKS is the world's leading
independent publisher of children's books.
Working with the best authors and illustrators
we create books for all ages, from babies
to teenagers – books your child will
grow up with and always remember. So…

FOR THE BEST CHILDREN'S BOOKS,
LOOK FOR THE BEAR